WHY DO MEN
DIE ON ME

WHY DO MEN DIE ON ME

J. CAROL GOODMAN

iUniverse, Inc.
Bloomington

WHY DO MEN DIE ON ME

This is a work of fiction. All of the characters, names, incidents, organizations, and dialogue in this novel are either the products of the author's imagination or are used fictitiously.

iUniverse books may be ordered through booksellers or by contacting:

iUniverse
1663 Liberty Drive
Bloomington, IN 47403
www.iuniverse.com
1-800-Authors (1-800-288-4677)

ISBN: 978-1-4620-6170-9 (sc)
ISBN: 978-1-4620-6171-6 (ebk)

Printed in the United States of America

iUniverse rev. date: 12/21/2011

This book is dedicated to Logan, Charity, Walter, Elisabeth, Tay, Ebbe, Emon, Clem, Sofie and Cal who make me abundantly happy

For Ted

Who encouraged me to create, waste time and be myself

LILY

$\mathcal{I}$was immediately attracted to him, the tall, lumbering man, with soiled and listing tennis shoes. His hair was slipping casually over his forehead and his out of style glasses had escaped down his nose as he displayed an inattentive ease. This man would someday be my daughter's killer.

He stepped off the porch of the Bluehill Inn in the Catskills to mill about with other guests on the lawn before dinner. As if he knew I was watching him he turned and looked at me, faintly smiling. I turned my back on my excitement. What silly fantasy was I having? I had never strayed from my marriage and wasn't about to, besides I was there with my parents and my two children.

For a number of years we had been going to the Inn in August, but not my husband. He went nowhere, except to the grocery to pick up a six-pack. When I smiled back at the man my parents didn't see me. My mother was picking at a wayward thread on her pongee blouse and Dad was talking to some men about the Yankee baseball game. Then one of the men brought up the Vietnam

1

War and said he had a friend whose son was fighting and didn't like how people were beginning to doubt why we were there. Dad said, "Not good. Not good." For me the war seemed far away. But I was aware of how different I'd feel if I'd had a son old enough to fight.

The man turned again to look at me. His smile showed a gap between his front teeth, which made him seem charming and harmless. I wondered if he were alone and what he was doing there.

My ten-year-old son, Don, was being his usual pain, jumping about, and climbing over the porch rail. I called to him to stop but he paid no attention. He lost his balance and tumbled into the flowerbed. Down the steps I raced to pull him out but the man had already righted Don. I thanked him as I tried to fluff up the mashed cosmos.

How would I get to talk to him with my hovering parents? I had never been a flirt and I hadn't questioned that I was happily married, with the routines that tied and encircled me in comfort. I wasn't interested in the sexual revolution or any revolution. When I heard my women friends complain that their husbands didn't help with the dishes or take care of the children, I thought, so what. He was earning the living wasn't he?

The dining hall had pine paneling, open log beams and rustic chairs around tables for six. Incongruous were the white tablecloths and Spode china with strawberry designs. On the walls hung prints of men in hip boots fishing in a flowing stream or scenes of icy winter banks with deep blue shadows. I had loved those serene pictures, but that evening they seemed dull.

My daughter Sally arrived just in time for dinner. Her fox colored hair, darker from her lake swim, was pulled neatly into a ponytail. She had often been solitary, exploring the pinewoods that had lost their undergrowth, and along the creek that fed the lake to watch frogs leap from the rocks. But almost eighteen she no longer went anywhere alone, whispering secrets with her huddling girlfriends and boyfriends. She seemed not to have anyone special yet. Often after dinner, across the darkness, their bubbles of laughter came in uncontrollable waves.

I couldn't help myself, I looked for the man. Had he left? Checked out? Then I saw him coming toward our table. I became agitated as if I were guilty of acting upon my hidden desire. He came straight to me and leaned over. My parents were staring. My children were staring. Had he read my mind? My face surged red in panic.

"Excuse me, did you lose your camera?" He laid my camera on the table next to me. He noticed my shaking hand as I picked it up.

To my surprise my father asked him if he were alone and would like to join us. My father had an engaging manner and loved to talk. My mother was friendly, but cautious, pinching her eyes to grasp a person's pedigree, looking for old money or aristocracy to count on. I could tell she disliked him. The man's name was William Densmore. "No, they don't call me Bill."

"Lily Barley, "he repeated, shaking my hand. "Musical name. Good choice." He winked at my parents and sat across from me acting a little too jolly.

My mother still squinting asked him, "Where are you from?"

But either he didn't hear her or he decided not to answer. I wondered if his jolly mood was a smoke screen for feeling uneasy. He laughed at a silly joke my father told him about golf. He said that he was known to play golf and tennis.

Dad looked a little puzzled. "Known to?"

But William just laughed and waved a hand. Sally asked him to pass the butter. She spread it carefully over her corn, sitting straight up as if for her portrait but her eyes remained indirect, not too interested in anyone above her age. He asked her, "What's you favorite subject in school?"

"Gym," she answered and I smiled knowing she hated gym. Her answer seemed to do exactly what she wanted, not to converse with him.

After dinner we strolled to the porch, William with us. Don skidded ahead, wired more than ever after nourishment. He had jumped up from the table a couple of times, seeing something out the window. Like his father Harlan, Don never ate a full meal with us.

Harlan would sit in the living room on the ugly leather chair he wouldn't let me throw away, with his feet on the torn ottoman, the only thing he inherited from his mother. He sat sucking on his beer, watching football, baseball, basketball on TV until he fell asleep.

The children and I sat in the dining room without him. Candle light, to make a genteel atmosphere, beautiful linen, fresh flowers. I was trying to teach them manners and how to have polite conversation.

When our meal was over Harlan grabbed Don and started rough housing, knocking over furniture, getting him wild with laughter and then to the point of crying. I yelled at them but afraid to go into their fracas. Fearless Sally rushed in, pulling at the bucking broncos and yelling, "Daddy, stop." And then she would wrench Don from him. When Don asked me years later, "Why did you always let Sally save me? Why didn't you?" I told him I wasn't brave.

We stepped off the porch to look at the red sunset.

Sally said, "Know what? I think of life as red or blue."

"The meaning?" William asked.

My mother interrupted, "Your father and I will take Don up to bed." Don turned and stuck his tongue out at us as he hopped up the stairs to the bedrooms. My father kept saying," calm down," in a low don't-cause-attention voice, he used on his distressed patients.

"I'm not sure," Sally continued, "Something to do with destiny. For instance red is death by fire and blue is dying alone."

I had never heard her talk like this.

"Happy thoughts," William said.

She smiled and shrugged her shoulders. But I remembered and sorry I remembered.

The photograph of my mother on my father's desk was a studio portrait of an imperious woman with her mink coat fanned out over her shoulders and across her lap in rich display. It was a photograph of a coat, a photograph of money and a photograph of a little girl who never grew up. They both also wanted me to be that little girl, and were even glad that I married my childhood playmate.

But you might think they wouldn't approve of Harlan, him being poor, from an uneducated family and Catholic, of all things, *not* Episcopalian. But they liked Harlan. He was smart and landed scholarships to college and graduate school and they were thrilled when right after his PhD in chemistry he was hired by a big laboratory in New Jersey, where we lived.

After we were married my mother tried to sit next to Harlan when we went to dinner at their house. She loved that Harlan was forever. There had been no divorces in our family. If there had been, like distant cousins, they were hushed up. She treated Harlan like a son, well not exactly, since my brother Talbot was her favorite.

Our wedding was disgustingly lavish. (Mother helped Harlan's mother buy the *right* dress and my father rented a tux for his father). I had thought then that lavish was wonderful. When my father kissed me afterwards, his kiss was lavish too. He kissed me more passionately than Harlan ever had. My father's lips were tender and sure. Harlan's were dry and quick. But what did I know? Harlan had been my only boyfriend since eighth-grade.

Almost anything turned me on. I knew only the basics about sex. My girlfriends and I didn't talk about sex, only love. When I figured out I wanted more imagination and wanted to talk about more satisfaction he snapped, "Lily, lack of satisfaction is your fault. You're an uptight Wasp."

For a long time I believed him, when of course he was the uptight one and wanted standard sex with the lights out, under the covers and even wanted that less and less . . . while I suppressed my longing. I bought an extravagant see-through nightgown, silk with rosebuds embroidered at the décolletage neck and lace underwear. He hardly noticed. He scorned me when I questioned where he was going, as he slithered out the door at night. He yelled, "What the hell did I marry? A prying wife?"

I made myself not care. I had wonderful children and they came first. I always tried to be attentive to them even as my subconscious was slipping sideways into deep longing and escape.

William turned to Sally and then to me and asked if we would like to walk up the hill behind the Inn to have a better look at the sunset. We followed him and just before the sun disappeared behind the softly rounded mountain he asked if he could take a picture of us. I turned suddenly to get the sun out of my eyes and my earring snagged on his shirt, pulling him to a halt as my head was yanked against his shoulder. We both tried to pull me free.

"If you kneel down," Sally said, "I can get at it better." Kneeling there my head against his shoulder seemed like a ceremony, a blessing. Sally slipped her finger tips in and we were free. As we stood up he looked at Sally as if he were seeing her for the first time. Then she ran off to find her friend to play ping-pong. He never took the picture.

William and I walked on around the lake. We came to the picnic tables and he reached into the outdoor fireplace for a piece of charcoal, took my hand and drew something in my palm. I laughed at the tickling. He pulled me to a light on the path and I saw that he had sketched a lily.

"I like your name. Lilies survive in all soils and weather. The only thing they need is sunshine."

What did he mean? Was he indicating he would be that sunshine in my life?

Of course not

The next day he was gone. I saw him out my bedroom window packing his car. He hadn't said goodbye. But why should I have been shocked? It hadn't been anything in the first place.

What lingered along with the shame of my desire for him was the night before he had asked me about my life and I told him that I took care of my house and kids, played tennis a bit, went to the movies with my girlfriends and read myself to sleep.

My life sounded so dull tears blossomed in my eyes. I had never thought about my life, just lived in the daily tasks. A few friends were beginning to get jobs, but Harlan had said, "Don't you dare. That would be the biggest insult . . . like I can't support you."

William had told me he worked for the government in a new field called Environmental Science and he checked out streams and lakes. He also told me he had never married and was sorry he didn't have children.

Back home I didn't want to but I thought about Talbot. My brother was fourteen and I was seven. Because it was the maid's night off my mother in particular decided he was old enough to care for me.

That was fine with me. My big brother, my protector when neighborhood kids got into scraps with me.

"It's bath time," Talbot said.

He shut the door and turned on the water and undressed me.

Was it fifteen minutes or was it hours? He washed me and then started over again. I said that I wanted to get out. He said I was not clean. He sprayed me with water again. I screamed, let me out. You aren't clean he hollered back. "I want to get out."

"If you stop screaming I will sing to you afterwards."

He lifted me out. I was shaking as if he were a stranger. He wrapped me in a towel and said, "Pretend you're a puppy, pretend you're a kitty." He gave me little bites across my belly making we laugh until I pulled away. "Stop," I said.

He put on my nightgown and he lifted me into bed. When he shut the door I cried with abandon. He had frightened me. I didn't understand why he would treat me with meanness like other big brothers I had heard of. I was ashamed that he had overpowered me, imprisoned me. My brother, my protector.

If I told my parents I believed they would think I was exaggerating or see nothing wrong. But the next time he offered to baby sit me I had a tantrum, pretending I would miss my parents too much if they went out. Although puzzled, they gave in and Talbot never offered again. I think he worried I would tell them. After that he avoided me or was mean, put me down every chance he could. And he left me with a lack of trust in the men I loved.

Maybe that was why I married Harlan. I thought he was the opposite from Talbot.

I thought he was distant, admiring me, putting me on a pedestal. He loved my looks, called me Madam X "with your patrician, profile," he said. He loved my black hair so I dyed the bits of gray. He poured out extravagant compliments fast and furious like a rash of obscenities, like bombastic swear words, those furious words of love . . . as if in battle. Words he didn't act upon. Words thrown out to the air, meaningless as far as real intimacy.

I tried to get William out of my mind. But I thought of nothing else. On a Saturday, two weeks later, the phone rang. Harlan picked it up.

"It's for you, a mister Wilcox."

He had found my number.

"Yes?" I said, business like . . . with my heart going nuts.

"I'm calling to ask you to lunch."

"No, I'm not interested in a home demonstration of a vacuum cleaner. I have a perfectly good one."

9

Sally had walked in the room. Did she hear a male voice on the phone?

"Please don't hang up," he said, "I just want to know if Monday is okay."

I paused. "No, I'm really not interested."

"I'll pick you up at the Grand Union parking lot in Bridgetown. Far left in back . . . twelve thirty."

I hung up. I hoped I wouldn't go.

Monday I was still hoping. Then I decided I would just meet him to explain why I couldn't see him. Meet him to be polite. I also decided to appear unattractive and put on an old ratty dress. I wore no makeup. Let him see I was not what he wanted. He would even be embarrassed to take me to a restaurant.

Turns out a restaurant was not what he had in mind and he didn't seem to notice my dress. Turns out I never explained why I couldn't see him. He said he was taking me to a surprise place. I thought, am I crazy? I don't even know this man. I was shaking as I stepped into his car. Nobody knew where I was. He could kill me and who would suspect him? And look at the insane way he was driving. Who was this man who loved the earth and drove to kill? My hands were sopping wet.

"You are so silent,"

"I guess I'm afraid of your driving."

He laughed as if I'd made a joke. But he slowed down a little.

I didn't ask him where we were going. I was too terrified of the answer. When he stopped, I thought, I will jump out and run for it. "Here we are." He swung into the park I knew well, between our two towns and where I often walked with my friend Trish. Because it was a weekday and early September not many people were in sight.

"Is this okay?" he asked.

The fact that he asked calmed me a little. He pulled out a World War II army blanket from the trunk and said it was his father's. "They sent it home after he was killed." He spread it out not far from where people walked on a path. That also gave me some comfort.

I sat down. "Where was your father?" Trying to make my voice normal.

"France. Soldiers were running into battle and one knocked him down by mistake and his arm hit a rock and broke. Infection set in. Ten days later he died. It never stops amazing me how being in a certain place at a certain time can be fatal . . . or marvelous.

He looked at me. And handed me the picnic basket he had brought and I opened. An expensive Sherry, Brie, which I had never tasted, French bread he kept hot on a brick and ripe pears. He poured the wine into crystal stemmed glasses.

He seemed unsure, asking me if everything was okay which made me more confident and charmed. We lingered over the meal. He wanted to know more about Sally, wondering if she were like me. Not at all, I told him. Social, outlandish and forthright. For dessert he opened a marble cake that he had baked. I had never know a man who cooked except on an outdoor grille.

"Come I'll show you something."

I'm not afraid, I kept reminding myself as he led me through bushes and to a brook. "This is one I've tested and found a shoe factory is pouring their waste into it. There are no more trout and it will be my job to get the government to stop them and make them clean it up."

"Do you like your work?"

"I'm passionate about . . ." his voice was loud and then too soft so that I was forced to lean close to hear, "about everything I pursue."

He knew by my smile how he affected me.

We turned back to our blanket. He said, "The last time I saw my father alive was at the Inn. That's why I went back there this year on his birthday. He took me there for a weekend to fish. I was nine. We caught three trout that day and we cooked the trout over the fireplace where I pulled out the charcoal to draw on your hand. You are lucky with your parents still alive."

"I'm not like my mother," is all I said.

"Which is?"

Before I could answer he looked at his watch and abruptly stood up. "I have to go." He rushed us toward the car. "I realized it was getting late and I have a meeting. By the way, you have a lovely daughter. I was taken with her . . . and your son too, quite a guy." I think he said that as an afterthought. Was it true he had to leave? Why had he not even tried to kiss me? Did he suddenly not like me?

He didn't say he would call. I was stunned with humiliation. When he swung into the parking lot and I said something like thank you for the nice time. He pulled out a calling card and said, "Please call me, either number." He must be dreaming. I never would call a man. We just didn't do that in those days.

Sally turned eighteen. Her hair was down beyond her shoulders, bouncing into light and dark as sunlight were skittering through a forest. She was such a responsible girl, perhaps even more so because her brother was off the scale.

She was steady and thoughtful. Watched when I needed something and picked up my very messy trail. And even the day of her birthday when she had four girlfriends over she insisted on cleaning up the dishes with me.

I was not going to call William, no sir. Almost two weeks had gone by. I went over every moment we had been together, looking for some clue or mistake. Not even a kiss on the cheek or telling me I was lovely, well, at least he said that Sally was lovely. I paced the floor with lemonade in hand. I swatted the cat. I didn't want to see William. I must see him.

Sally noticed something when she came home from school and she tried little sweetnesses to make me happy. This was the fall of her senior year. She handed me a picture from art class and I hung it in the kitchen. It was of a parade on Memorial Day. I thought it was an unusual subject. She handed me the mail.

I sorted through a bunch of junk, my foot on the garbage pedal. I dropped something I hadn't noticed, a letter to me written in an almost illegible sprawl. Inside was a small piece of white paper with an imprint of lips made with lipstick. It was a man's lips, broad, flat, large, with the mouth slightly open. I tucked the letter into my skirt pocket.

"What was that?" Sally asked.

"Nothing. Some silly lipstick advertisement."

"Why don't you throw it away?"

"Yes." I tore the letter and dropped it in, letting the lid bang shut.

I can't say how many weeks went by when I received a call from a nurse at the Ridgedale hospital. I knew it was him trying to disguise his voice.

I went along, "Oh my God, what happened?"

"A car accident. He's recovering. Fell off a cliff from inspecting a brook. Broken bones. He asked me to call you. Grand Union parking lot in fifteen minutes."

Harlem looked up, "Who was that?"

I thought fast. "I left some groceries at the store and they called me." I ran out.

His car was in a dark corner of the lot. I peered in the window to be sure it was William.

"I didn't know if you would come. I called you because I was worried."

"Worried about?"

"The calling card I gave you."-

"That it would get in the wrong hands?"

"Worried because you hadn't used it. Two weeks and a half, for godsake."

"I wasn't going to call. I waited for you."

"Did you like my lips?"

I didn't tell him I thought of nothing else. I could hardly run the house, buy groceries, the kids school shoes. I was too afraid to leave the house in case the phone rang.

"You were reluctant? Is it your marriage?"

"No, not really. I'm not brave."

"Sure you are. Look at you."

On the way home the guilt roared in, my husband, my children, yet I felt powerful, my first overwhelming sense of power. William had been thrilled at my body's willful aggressive response to him and I felt lightning had struck and crippled me as we kissed.

He said "the reason I didn't phone you was I wanted you to be sure."

William called from his office, once ducking out of a conference. He was somebody else each time in case I didn't pick up. Selling bulbs for the garden, asking for political donations or tennis dues and once to be funny when I answered, he said, oops, got the wrong number.

I put a long cord on the phone so I could easily grab it. We wrote letters too and hid them, no name, between the pages of an obscure book in the library which had not been taken out for years. *Women's Fashions in the Time of the French Rrevolution.*

"Don't ask," William said, as he blindfolded me. "This is in celebration of two weeks together." We drove for about a half an hour. Stopped. Got on some kind of tram. I wondered what people thought with me blindfolded. Nobody came up and said are you all right, or was I being abducted? Which I was.

Finally we stopped. "Will you promise to keep your eyes shut. I will take your hand." After a long walk with people's voices, people scurrying he said I could open my eyes. We were in an air terminal. "Stay here," he said and went to a short line and came back. "Gate 5."

"Wait a minute, where are you taking me? I can't run away."

"Don't you trust me?"

I didn't answer.

But if only I hadn't gotten more involved with him my daughter would be alive. One hour flight. We stepped off in Boston. Then a taxi. He had made a reservation for lunch at the harbor. "They are cleaning up the bay now at last. I wanted you to see what I'm working on."

I was so in love. This man flew me to Boston for lunch and afterwards we took a taxi to the Ritz Carlton.

Red silk sheets. And, so unlike myself, didn't mind kissing in public all through the lunch.

"Let's spend the night," he said.

"You know I can't."

"Make up something."

"Sure, like I happen to be in Boston, sorry can't get home tonight."

"He doesn't sound like he'd give a darn."

"He has a temper."

On the plane home we ate the peanuts and pretzels without talking, I think stunned by our ecstasy and our declarations and wondering how it would end.

"So where have you been?" Sally asked.

"Tea with Trish."

Harlan looked up from the TV and said nothing.

"I wanted you to shop with me for sneakers," Sally said.

I didn't answer, but rushed into the bathroom to stop the conversation. When I came out and started boiling the pot for noodles, I noticed Don was amazingly quiet. He seemed on edge the way he was chewing his lip but didn't talk. His hair was long and my father told him it would be better if he didn't appear at the club like that, Don didn't mind, but my parents did. I have to admit that was the first I noticed how unkempt Don looked. I shrugged my shoulders after he paid no attention to me. I wasn't concentrating on my children.

And I certainly didn't think, this is Sally's last year home. She would be going half way across the country to the University of Chicago next fall.

I was about to go meet William when who walks up to the door but my father. I hadn't seen my parents for a while. He looked very handsome, tall, straight spined, sparkling with energy. When I was little he was my best friend. He paused no matter what to give me attention when he noticed I needed some. He would never be direct, ask what was the matter but just distract me with affection.

"Cookie, darling. I won't take but a minute."

"That's okay. I'm not in a hurry. I was just going to the grocery." I had never since I was a child, lied to him.

"Your mother and I were a little concerned about you."

I turned around and knocked over the hall lamp and it crashed into many pieces. He rushed to find the broom and dustpan ahead of me. When I was a child he could deal with anything, vomit, diarrhea. Hold me in his arms, while my mother took a walk.

He was trying not to look at what I was wearing, a peasant skirt from India with little mirrors everywhere and a revealing tight blouse. I no longer went to the beauty parlor. William liked my hair lose and wild. He had given me orange papier-mâché bird earrings from Mexico, which were flipping about as if flying.

"I've come to tell you I've made you and Harlan members of the country club. An anniversary present."

"A present?" I asked with a swallow. "Thank you . . ." tears were forming in the back of my throat. I knew I wasn't part of his life anymore and I wanted to be honest, tell him about William.

"Dad that was nice. But you won't feel bad about Harlan. He likes to stay home. Doesn't do anything with me."

"I know, dear."

Perhaps I told him in case he found out about William and me, let him know, what Harlan looked like from the inside. "Harlan likes a new beer from Yugoslavia. He sits in that chair. He takes white bread and rolls a slice into little knots and stuffs it in with his gulping beer. He sleeps in the attic room. His choice because he stays up so late. I went up once to clean it. He was furious. Told me never to come again. It is hard for me to describe the mess. It was all over, dirty clothes all over the place, beer bottles."

"Well," Dad said. He looked at the floor. He cleared his throat. I waited for him to console me. But he made a vague gesture as if a bug were skimming across his face. "Sorry. I didn't mean to keep you, dear. You'll get the membership card in the mail. Maybe you and I could play tennis."

I stopped him. "I did want to tell you I have some good news."

"Yes?" He smiled at me.

I was going to blurt out about William. Certainly he would understand. I was looking straight into his eyes, the blue of which had faded with age.

"I'm very happy," was all I could explain.

"Oh I know that. I can tell," he said with what I imagined was a certain shared secretiveness between us. I wanted to tell him that William was the first man from whom I had known real love, not just extravagant words of love that Harlan still poured out at me with no substantiation. Yet I was sad for our lost youth and the blamelessness of childhood we had together.

William became really nervy and began to stop by our house after work saying if Harlan walked in he'd explain we had met at the Inn. Then I noticed he arrived just as Sally came home from school. Sally began to hang around, not going up to her room to study as usual. I made coffee and served cookies. I don't know how it started, but the Vietnam War came up. There was to be a big demonstration against it in D.C.

William said to her, "Lets go." I felt almost as a second thought he said, "The three of us."

He came to our house to bring us the flyers. Don was just coming home from school. He greeted us and went upstairs.

"He's acting like an old man," William whispered.

"Yeah?" which made me feel like a bad mother.

"But, I was like Don at that age."

"Which was?" Sally asked, her voice brightening whenever he was around.

"Oh stumbling around."

"Can't imagine you like that," she said.

"I had no clue what I was doing on this earth until I read Rachel Carson's book, *Silent Spring*. That was the beginning of my intense interest. Because my father died in a war I want to help stop this war."

"Me too," she said, though I had never heard her care.

In D.C the crowd was huge, stretching out along the mall. Young and old, wheel chairs and baby carriages, singing. *Where have all the flowers gone?* Picnics were hauled out, sharing with strangers, milling about. Vendors wove in and out. When Bella Abzug poured out her heart the crowd sat and listened. Sally had made a sign, MAKE LOVE NOT WAR. Sally's face was blissful. She reached for William's hand and briefly squeezed it. I thought, how nice, along with a twinge.

All I could think of doing with Sally was to buy her clothes. Was I turning into my own mother? Sally's darkening chestnut hair was now a vine of twisted curls on the narrow shoulders. Her breasts and lips were plumply luscious and her cheeks still round from childhood. To dress her was a worshiping task. Her skin was soft as warm butter. But she changed her attitude toward clothes. Turned up in worn blue jeans and T shirts.

William took her to every demonstration that came up. I was invited, but didn't always go. Fair Housing, barber shops that wouldn't cut black people's hair, nuclear plants. They organized a candle-light vigil on our town green and read the names of the dead. I watched them carefully. Sally was changing radically in ways I couldn't face. She was not as congenial with me and was testy at times. *Let me decide, leave me alone.*

I became obsessed with her. She was noisy and hasty, flamboyant and clumsy knocked things off the counter, off the table as she turned the corner, saying upps and giggling. Her presence had the excitement of a discovery about to happen.

It was spring. William found a hill, secluded, he thought. He liked to make the gourmet lunches, loved being fully prepared, the chilled wine, the army blanket, mosquito spray and even a sickle. I always wore a skirt for easy access and he changed into old shorts that he kept in a briefcase in the trunk. We had just finished making love when a horseman coming out of the woods a few yards away said, "Couldn't you find somewhere else to do that?"

When he left I said, "I know that man. He goes to our club. I don't know his name and he doesn't know mine."

But we giggled. When I told my friend Trish she said, "When the little guy comes up the head goes in the sand."

I noticed that Sally seemed to have given up most of her friends unless they went with William and her. I tried to squash my growing jealousy. He and Sally sat on the couch talking endlessly about the Vietnam War. I knew for certain she was in love. And him? Yet William told me all the time how much he loved me, that I was his life . . . was this a mixed message? That didn't necessarily mean he couldn't love two people.

Sally said, "What you say we all go back to the Bluehill Inn before I go to college. We can hand out anti-Vietnam war leaflets."

She and William had designed them and they went off for half a day to print them over at his place.

I wondered if she had persuaded her father to come so she could see more of William, that she thought I would have to pay attention to Harlan. I couldn't believe that Harlan said yes when he never went anywhere. But I knew he and Don would be watching football on the TV. At the Inn William arranged our rooms far apart, in case . . .

"In case ?"

"Wait and see."

Don and Sally each had their own rooms. I usually didn't bother looking at Harlan but there at the Inn I was painfully aware. He was fat and wasted both. His nose was telltale red of a drinker and he didn't shave on vacation and I wondered if we would be asked to leave, but it was hippy time and people were getting used to long hair in men, beards and very casual attire. Yet I felt both ashamed . . . and sorry for Harlan.

He was talkative to the milling pre-supper crowd, crowing about how proud he was of Sally getting into the University of Chicago. He was very drunk, but more than that, by late evening I knew what William's plan was but I wasn't exactly sure it would work. William invited us to his room for a nightcap of whisky.

Later I made sure that Harlan was snoring before I rushed out to meet William, my desire so excruciating that my toes felt numb. William had sneaked a sleeping pill in Harlan's night cap, but Harlan was a restless sleeper, so I was nervous. The night was black and I had to hold tightly to the rail to find my way down the steps and across the lawn. When William heard me coming he flashed his light so I could see my way along the narrow ledge on either side of a docked canoe in the boathouse. The moon teased its way from under the clouds just enough for fleeting glimpses of our mirrored faces. I wore my shortest skirt and top. We had to lean against the boathouse wall, forcing our crushed bodies into bliss, as the licking, sloshing water, chanted with our murmurs.

Back home the next day in the morning I had just put the phone down from William and my review of the night before when Harlan came through the door from work and slammed down his briefcase. As though shot in the back his whole weight fell on me slamming me against the door. Taking my shoulders he slammed me again. Sally heard and jumped down the stairs yelling and throwing books at her father. She plunged at him like a boxer, strong and lithe as he continued to slam me against the door. "Stop it," she screamed, pulling him away, like the great Viking that she was.

"If you are in love with that hippy jerk I'll kill you both."

"No you won't," Sally said.

I never knew if the man on the horse ratted on us.

"Oh yes I will."

I did not tell Harlan where I had moved. Soon William moved in with me and so did Sally. Not Don. I gave my telephone number to Don and asked him not to tell his father. Don acted like nothing had changed in his life. And Sally, sometimes feeling my conflict of guilt, would say you did the right thing, Mom. She and William would sit up late, he helping and discussing her homework when I was asleep. I couldn't believe, wouldn't face what might be happening. I felt terrible that I couldn't wait until she went to college. But when William crawled into bed we made love . . . though was he thinking of her?

I only saw my mother and father at the club for lunch and this way the conversation could be bland, almost harmonious, and I was even amused at my mother and what used to gall me, her incessant trivial talk about every person who went by.

Lolly Persons had to get a new yacht otherwise she couldn't join the Bermuda race this year. Brandan Lowell finally had no choice but to buy an apartment in Paris. He also has one in London where work takes him. He's such a domestic type, can't stand hotels . . .

When William and I took Sally to the airport for the University that fall she fell into his arms and they kissed on the lips. When she kissed me I saw that she had tears in her eyes from their embrace. I didn't dare look at his eyes.

23

She wrote separate letters to William and to me. But we read each other's letters.

To him she wrote she was forming group to work on peace demonstrations. To me she wrote about her studies, her friends. To Don and Harlan she described the football games and later basketball and told Don that lots of kids there had pony tails like him. William and I wrote separate letters to her, mine domestic, his political except phrases I read as messages. The demonstrations are not the same without you. I miss you terribly, my sweet.

The day the war ended we shouted to one another in happiness. William told me he had called her when I was out. He told her she had helped end the war.

On April 27, 1970 William received a letter, *William I wish you could come protest with me at Kent State. They are protesting where the school wants to put a gym on that hill where all those students were killed for protesting the war. You were the one who set me on the path. You are my inspiration. I wish you could come. Will you come? I send you all my love. Sally*

That night I looked over at William as we lay naked on our bed. He was silent. I couldn't bear his going as he stood up to dress. I thought that she was safely half a continent away. I wasn't going to follow him. He put the same worn sneakers he had when I first met him. He put a few clothes in a suitcase. He came to kiss me goodbye.

"But it will be all kids."

"I don't want to disappoint Sally."

I was sick.

I watched him dress. I couldn't believe. He packed a small suit case and was putting on his shoes when the phone rang.

"No, she is right here." He handed the phone to me.

"This is sergeant Miller. Is this Mrs. Baily?

"Yes."

"Is your daughter Sally?"

"Yes."

"I'm sorry to tell you . . ." he stopped to get his breath, "Your daughter? Sally Baily has had an accident."

"Is she hurt? What kind of accident?"

"She was driving. Sorry, very . . ."

"Hurt? Is she hurt?"

"She was so beautiful," his voice broke.

My memory hardly holds the details. Fell asleep, down a ravine, hit a tree.

Driving through the night to get to Kent State. Only seven more miles to go.

Was it the tree? No she fell out and farther down a ravine, already gone when the EMS arrived. Instant death, the police tried to console. She had no pain . . . all pain transferred to me and Harlan and Don and William.

I didn't have the strength to consol my parents. At first I didn't know why they hadn't consoled me. I realized all the consoling for myself had to be done by me and I could not rely on myself to help me in my devastation. I was a charred shadow.

I went to cry with my parents. When I left my father followed me out, and seeing tears falling down my face he took out his handkerchief and wiped them, as he had done so often when I was a child. Don tried to comfort me too, just coming to the little house that William and

I bought and bring me cookies and chocolate and sit holding my hand as we said nothing.

At Harlan's and my old house Sally's room had been left with many things from her childhood, dolls and stuffed animals, ribbons from horseback riding, anti-war buttons and the poster *Make love not war*, shelves of books and makeup, which she had given up, scarves hanging on the back of the door, tiny Japanese lanterns hanging from the ceiling and a framed picture of her girlfriends and her at her eighteen's Birthday. In her closet was a velveteen bathrobe she never wore that my mother had given her one Christmas, two pairs of old bluejeans, a spring coat and five abandoned dresses. My friend Trish helped me pack boxes for the Salvation army. I threw away an unfinished letter she had written William. It started, *Dear William, I love.* nothing more. Don put the pictures into three albums and gave one to Harlan, one to me and one to my parents.

I never opened mine. I thought if I did I might bleed to death.

I know the moment I felt an aversion toward William two or three weeks later. He disgusted me when he chewed. He made noises when he cut his meat and slurped his coffee. I began to despise him. I enjoyed despising him. After dinner one night he followed me into the living room. "Lily . . ." he said.

"I'm busy, I can't talk."

When he started to put his arms around me I panicked. He could feel my heaving and that I was about to faint. He pulled away. At night we lay side by side. I could feel him holding himself still, careful not to destroy what was left of me, not to lean against my scars or peel away my burned skin . . . that I began to realize he had caused.

"Lily, you have got to talk to me."

"I can't stand you anymore."

"Why?"

"You don't know? You killer. To think I ever loved my daughter's killer."

He sat up in bed, turned on the light and looked at me.

"You led her like a lamb to . . ."

"Lily, I would have taken her place and you know that." He pounded his pillow.

"Instead she died for you. And for what reason?"

"Not for me. She wanted a different world filled with peace."

"Oh, my God," I said, with the screams of hatred. "You killer."

The next day William came home from work early. As he came up the sidewalk the UPS man caught up with him and handed him a package for me. I saw that it was from the police in Kent State. William stood next to me as I cut the package open. "Do you mind?" I said, and moved through the hall, the kitchen, to the back door and down the steps to the back yard. I pulled out something made of cloth with straps. It was Sally's daypack and the note inside said, "Sadly I send you what we found of your daughter's possessions in the car. Ohio State Police."

I stood against the tall privet hedge. I heard William come out. But I was too engrossed, too much with Sally to care. I pulled out her red sweater and rubbed my cheek against it, breathing her scent. I folded it and laid it on the grass. Her purse had five dollars and some coins thrown lose, a chapstick, her soft hairbrush with strands of her red hair. I laid the brush on the grass. I pulled out a pair of lavender socks and undid the knot and laid them on the sweater. Near the bottom was a half empty bottle of water.

I had not heard William stepping closer. I reached down to the last item. Something firm and slick. I pulled out a green apple. I turned to look at him. I saw that he was familiar, like someone who has been away a long time. I squinted to put him back into my memory, to explain who he was. I saw that he was still a young man, clumsy, his glasses falling down his nose. Some one I had once known.

When he was beside me I showed him the apple. I took my thumb nail and arduously split the apple in two. I put half in my left hand and half in my right as though on a scale, as though to remember their weights. He watched me as I ate core and all.

"I want you to go." I said with strength, as though her energy. "Now. Go."

I picked up Sally's belongings, turning each over and gazing in wonder that there was not one dent in the water bottle. I put the items back in her daypack. I stepped toward my house that looked only vaguely familiar and I heard the uneven steps of William following me.

"Go. Get out right now. I don't want to see you. Not ever again. You killed her."

"Please, I love you. We can help each other."
I screamed until he packed his car and left.

Months passed. William tried calling. I slammed the phone down. I saw my mother and father and Don as he came like a ghost to eat or sleep. My friend Trish tried to coax me out and said she would not give up.

August was hot. I cared about nothing and vaguely wondered if my life would be like this forever. I heard a knock. I didn't answer knocks. My family just came in. The knock went on with such persistence I opened it.

"No."

I tried to shut him out but he was too strong. I jumped back as William came in and shut the door. I was screaming and backing up, but he kept on coming, his arms spread wide, spread out like great engulfing wings. I backed away, down the hall until I backed into the wall, and he was almost next to me and there was no place else for me to go.

The End

THE DEVINE COMEDY

*J*ust before dawn Hazel sneaked the rickety suitcase onto the bed of her Basement apartment. Two years ago her daughter, Jessica, found the suitcase in the dump when she forced Hazel to pack up her apartment and move in with her. If Jessica and her stupid husband heard her leaving they would swoop like limber spiders to snag her in her tracks.

Quietly she laid in a few plain clothes suitable for the task, dung colored pants from the hippy era, two white dresses for the pure, innocent look, and blue jeans for travel . . . oh and one nightgown without sleeves, which could double as a dress in very hot weather. Among her clothes she placed her sculpture tools, although when would she have the chance to use them? She dragged the suitcase on the rug to the door, wondering if the rickety thing would hold up.

Without wheels it would be heavy and painful on her arthritic back and she would have to move slowly. She remembered and tiptoed up the stairs to her daughter's kitchen where she always ate breakfast earlier than Jessica, a late riser because of her all night disgusting activities. Hazel ate lunch and dinner alone also, couldn't stand the boring husband Jessica had been forced to marry. No children. They probably never slept together. She *hoped* they never slept together, the idea of that man's boulder-body, thick hands, lips that splattered words all over the place gave Hazel the shivers. Anyway they couldn't have children now that her daughter was over fifty.

Hazel grabbed a pile of Jessica's leaflets from the kitchen counter, stuffing them in her worn pocketbook, from the days one could still buy endangered turtle skin.

Now came the saddest moment, saying goodbye forever to her life's work, *The Devine Comedy.* She gently caressed each, the gigantic ones she had carved in marble, eight and ten feet tall standing along the basement walls. Reaching as far as she could she ran her gnarled fingers over their faces and the map of their naked bodies. The grapefruit sized ones of alabaster, sitting on a shelf by her one small window, gave off a greenish translucent light that she felt was spiritual.

In the darkest corner sat the tortured figures curled in the agony of *hell.* When she had carved their twisted bodies, her fingers and knuckles ached in sympathy. She could not touch the three in *purgatory,* hanging from the ceiling, to say goodbye.

She kissed the two cameos on her night table, tiniest figures from *paradise* she called her babies, small enough to nestle in the palm of her hand. In those days her hands were as agile as a pianist.

These were her memoir, her diary. She also had risen from *hell* to *paradise* and for this moment *purgatory.*

Squelching a moan, she lingered with the one she could hardly bear to leave, the life-size marble of her and her lover. She stroked the two Venetian marble figures, closed her eyes to memorize their exquisite secret flesh, their faces in the deliverance of love . . . legs circling each other, her and her lover's head thrown back, pale veins beneath their chins, her finely chiseled hair cascading over their half closed lids. Although Hazel hadn't seen him for four years she knew he still lived in town. His name appeared in the byline as art critic in the San Francisco Daily. And she still longed for him.

She minced open the door. Jessica would be mad as a wet hen when she discovered Hazel had cut her clothesline to fashion a handle on the suitcase. What the hell, Jessica's fault, too cheap to buy a dryer. She couldn't take a last look at the children of her creation. She shut the door, holding back her tears.

The bus to San Francisco would come in fifteen minutes and she mustn't miss it. She tried to hurry but the going was stiff and painful on the uneven cement sidewalk. A desolate area with vacant fields or monstrous houses set back from the road. Sunday was the only day she wasn't lonely because she and her younger daughter met. It used to be that Avis came to her sculpture classes she had taught on Saturdays but Hazel had given up her students or rather they had given her up, too far away from where she used to live. And also Jessica had forbidden Avis to enter her house ever again.

Now 7:00. A.m. the bus would arrive at 7:02. Her heart was thumping with the strain but mostly from fear of being caught if her daughter woke and rushed out to find her. She never left until noon and the clothesline cut and the suitcase, that always sat in the corner, gone.

Jessica could get a court order. She could call Hazel incompetent, her age, her history.

It had been another bad night for Hazel. She was tired. How could she sleep hearing all the sobbing and screaming most nights where Jessicas locked them in her den? Hazel gritted her teeth, feeling the gut pain, even after all these years, of what her daughter was up to. But because Hazel's money was gone. She had had to live with her.

After many hours all would be quiet and the victim would be given hot milk and locked in the guest bedroom for some sleep. That was the first step. Then Jessica kept it up for days until the victims were thoroughly brainwashed. Fed them, spoke encouraging words to them. Exhausting work. Even with her success Jessica had frown groves in her smooth face, her eyes darted as if scanning for more and more in the jungle of sin. But Hazel felt Jessica's eyes hardened at the sight of her mother whom she had not won over along with Avis.

Hazel spotted the bus at a distance and tried to go faster, despairing that she had once had a straight back and that she had been tall and popular with men who commented on her vibrant looks, her sexy walk. Yet as she had shrunk her vision had become sharper and more discerning. She stored away tiny details of faces and parts of bodies, a hand, an eyebrow or curve of an ear for her art.

The bus squeaked its brakes and the door opened. A man stepped off and seeing Hazel struggle toward him he helped her lift her suitcase. She put on a Southern accent, "I depend on the kindness of strangers." He smiled and really noticed her. She turned her expert charm on him, a full smile with all her teeth still nicely assembled . . . and wondered if he had unveiled her long ago beauty.

She sat in the back of the bus and shut her eyes. Maybe she could snooze, get her energy back. But her mind heard the wailing and she wondered again how she could have a daughter so different. But she looked the most like Hazel with her rusty curly hair, patrician forehead, Hazel's mother had pronounced. But Jessica had a larger bosom, a sort of one-piece shelf, that reminded Hazel of bumpers on the electric cars at Asbury Park in New Jersey, where she had taken the girls on Sundays.

Jessica's voice was softer, perfect for hypnotizing, with its captivating soothing hospice quality . . . *Death* was what Hazel felt about Jessica's sessions, imprisoning the floundering young. Wasn't it ironic that she was going to use Jessica's leaflets in order to free Avis and herself?

She did feel guilty, should have left Jessica a better note than, *see you later.* See you later was a lie. She would never return. But she would write her from unknown places, call her now and then. It was not in Hazel's nature to be cruel.

Jessica was so busy she hardly noticed her anyway . . . except to say. "We must sell the kiln. I can't afford the electricity and there is no room anyway for more big Pieces. It's not like people are clamoring for them." Hazel turned away so the movers wouldn't see her destroyed face.

Jessica also took charge of her social security check, claiming she was forgetful now. Her check was deposited into a bank, but she had forgotten the name and Jessica had *something of attorney.* Gave her only a few dollars to go to town to see Avis and the rest of the money Jessica told her went for room and board and any clothes etc. etc.

And Avis had just enough to pay for the rented room and food from her SSI disability check. Although on Sunday Hazel brought her anything she could sneak out, a banana, pear, apple and a sweet. Avis was unable to hold a job, well didn't want a job anyway. She sometimes had to change pills and wait for her moods to vanish.

The bus ride was a difficult time for Hazel, seeing it all over again, the bus thirty years ago.

Jessica had stared at Bud and her out the bus window. "I'm shutting the door," the bus driver had said, "watch your hands. Get away." And another man shoved her and Bud away, nearly toppling Hazel as they tried to climb the steps to rescue her. The man jumped on the bus and the doors snapped shut.

The unmarked white bus filled with young people moved away. They ran after it, seeing Jessica's face pressed against the glass. Jessica waved goodbye, her expression confused, as if waking from a nap, her lips against the window, mouthing what they imagined was goodbye.

The hired a detective explained even if he found Jessica she was twenty-one and had her rights. The warehouse like building, that had briefly been Reverend Cloud's prison-home, was completely deserted after that, removing all his converts to a hidden place.

The fast talking, energetic private eye hunted as far as Chicago where it was rumored Cloud had another warehouse dormitory. Couldn't find it. He interviewed other detectives, interviewed other parents. No clues.

After Jessica left Hazel carved and molded more of Jessica's body into her pieces. Bud accused her of being just as much a religious nut as Jessica through her obsession with the *Devine Comedy*, though she had never been a church person that struck her as interesting. Her work became the source of hers and Bud's fighting. She thought of nothing else, and finally they divorced, now he was dead and never found out that Jessica was found. Avis, in high school, came into her studio after school and worked in clay. Her fingers were naturally clever and her weird outlook made her art original. Her subject was dogs. Dogs with their mouths wide open ready to attack. "Attacking what?" Hazel asked. Those in *hell*, in the *Devine Comedy* she told Hazel. From then on she and Avis tended to be on the same path. But a year after Jessica had disappeared Avis told Hazel religion scared the shit out of her, that's what the dogs meant.

Hazel had loved that Avis had come to carve in her studio in Jessica's house, actually The Reverend Cloud's house. He owned everything, and gave Jessica and her husband hardly enough to buy food. She often had to beg in the streets.

Avis's mostly unfinished or unresolved and abandoned work sat in the hall next to Hazel's bathroom, covered up with wet clothes to keep the clay from drying. Months had gone by because of Jessica not allowing Avis to enter her house ever again. Although Hazel was angry at Jessica she was afraid to express it, afraid Jessica would do something awful, get rid of her sculpture . . . put her in a home. But she kept on hoping Jessica would relent and let Avis back. Such a small thing Avis had done. When her sister and husband were out she made herself a sandwich for her trip back home and took some change from a jar. Jessica found out what was missing and told her that was a criminal and she was never to come inside her house again.

Nearly twenty years Jessica was out of their lives. She adored her older daughter and missed her everyday. After ten years she called. At first she thought it was a crank but then she recognized her voice.

"Where are you? We will come get you."

"Just wanted to know how you and Dad and Avis are?"

"Fine. Fine. Please. No, don't hang up."

"I'm only allowed one minute. I'll call again sometime."

After that she called every few months, telling them nothing. Only asking how they were and saying she was happy.

"Is it warm where you are?" She asked Jessica one time, trying anything to locate her and Jessica answered, "Yes, I'm in San Francisco."

"San Francisco, where? What address?" Jessica hung up.

Bud's words were slurred and cropped. He was retired and drinking and living across town. "Not me. I'm not going looking. Not today. Not tomorrow. She can fucking come to us."

"Maybe she can't. Maybe she's stuck, waiting, wanting us to rescue her. Maybe she's ill."

"I've spent half my life on this. Enough. It was *your* fault. All those unreal unearthly damned statues, giving her way-out notions on religion." He hung up. Hazel knew that Jessica had ruined his life.

Hazel bought a red van, Jessica's favorite color. She packed it with her sculptures and tools and even her kiln, let Bud move back in their house instead of insisting he should sell it and traveled with the little inheritance she had left. By the time Bud had died he had let the porch collapse and the roof leak into the bathroom, which rotted the floor so badly the tub fell through the ceiling landing onto the living room couch.

On the way she called Avis who at the time was living in New Hampshire with a backwoodsman. "I'm coming too. God the woods is dullsville."

Even if she couldn't find Jessica, San Francisco would take passed years of hell and purgatory over Jessica to maybe find Paradise. She drove across the country singing along with the radio. Hippy times and life seemed free and safe enough to sleep in parks. She drove on back roads lost her way several times. Strangers were kind. A couple invited her to sleep in their tent when it was raining. What a narrow life she had led. She really felt for the first time that the earth was round and she was turning with it.

She would go down every street knowing Cloud's flock begged in the streets.

One great anxiety remained, if she found her daughter would she recognize her after twenty years?

Jessica had been a difficult child, given to cranky disturbances and uncalled for tantrums. The only quick way to quiet her down was to give her chocolate candy. When she came home from college and found she had a B in chemistry, and her anger rocketed, even then chocolate seemed to work like a tranquilizing drug.

But it had to be the very best—dark Swiss chocolate. When she bit a piece off, she shut her eyes and released a little moan of calm and acted as if she might swoon. As far as Hazel knew she never bought candy for herself. Had to be from her mother.

Jessica insisted on going to India after college she was already seeking something. But when she was about to take the bus from NYC to the airport a sweet-talking woman coerced her into spending the night, "instead of sitting all night at the airport." She had called her parents to say goodbye and say where she was and they rushed to NYC, suspecting, knowing how Reverend Cloud captured disoriented young people to convert.

It was a dark night when Hazel reached San Francisco and had no idea where to go. She wouldn't check into a hotel afraid her art might be stolen. She was sitting in her van in a park with the window open and loudly crying, wondering what to do when a woman walking her dog heard her and offered her a place to stay until she found a place. She helped her find the row house apartment she then lived in for nearly eighteen years near Golden Gate Park. The woman remained her friend until she died. All her friends were dead or in a nursing home or gaga or moved to live with a son or daughter, just like her, freedom gone.

"The art you are doing is sacrilege," Jessica told her.

"What are you talking about?"

"Thou shalt not make graven images unto the Lord."

"They are not about God but about afterllife."

"You have no right to picture the mind of God."

"Artists have been doing that from the beginning of time."

"Yes, and art is where sin started."

"And she really said those things?" Avis had asked.

Now when the bus stopped in San Francisco she spotted Avis and ran to her arms. Leaning against a building she showed Avis what she had brought. "That's good. Jessica always goes out with white cups so I brought two. You look great, Mom. Even the food stain on the front of your dress and those I've-seen-better-times-sneakers."

Hazel didn't answer that she hadn't noticed the stain and her sneakers were the only sneakers she had for the last ten or so years.

"But we should empty your suitcase into my backpack."

They undid the suitcase right on the sidewalk leaving it at the curb. Avis pulled out two collapsible canvas stools that she had snatched from the backwoods boyfriend.

Sitting didn't work. People ignored their cups and leaflets."

"Let's go there." Hazel pointed to the intersection. When the light was red a few clinking coins were dropped in. But the air was hot and Hazel felt a little faint. By noon they counted $26.70. We need $200 to get to Salt Lake City.

"We have enough to buy two sandwiches. And maybe for some supper too."

Across at the park they found a vendor and a stand that sold flavored crushed ice. They sat under a Linden tree and ate their sandwiches slowly. "I bet Jessica won't miss me for days. She's so busy, frantic really. She doesn't have room for anything. The other day she couldn't even take me to my eye checkup. I had to take two buses, an all day trip."

They lay down in the park deciding if they didn't get enough money for a bus fare they would hitch-hike but the shady tree lured them to stay for a while. Avis said, "Tell me more about growing up rich." She fell back and looked at the sky, her long body looking like Ophelia, dressed in a Mumu of pinks and pale orange. She had picked a few petunias behind a *don't pick* sign and put them over her ears.

"Grandma died and my mother inherited a lot. I don't know how much. Then we moved to Connecticut into a huge house with three servants and my brother and me had one wing and my parents another. I walked along the shore collecting stones. I hid them from my brother who liked to destroy what I made. I guess I was nine or ten years old. I glued them together into designs and hid them under the big porch that jutted out toward the sound. But one day my brother found all eighteen and smashed them with a hammer. I hated him for many years but when he was dying in the hospital in Florida I flew to visit him and he told me that he was sorry for what he had done but glad that he hadn't stopped me from being an artist.

"That night in the hotel I stayed up and carved him a tiny amulet to save his life. But a week and a half later he was dead. The tiny angel I had carved in rose wood was under his pillow when he died."

Avis hugged her mother.

Hazel said, "Let's get a slice of pizza and hitchhike."

With pizza still in their mouths they got a ride on the back of a truck but were let off only a few miles down the road and they were nowhere with night falling. "We have water and a field to sleep in." As she lay in the warm night she hoped that Avis wouldn't have one of her spells, get unreal and act cuckoo. Well, she hadn't for a long time and she was particularly good when she had no stress, which was now, wasn't it? She took her daughter's hand. "Sleep tight, don't let the bugs bite."

As she drifted off she thought of her past lover.

Even before she moved to Jessica's she hadn't seen him for several years. Well, that wasn't quite true. She saw him at art openings that she could get to but he was distant toward her, sometimes pretending he didn't know her. She contemplated exposing him but that was revengeful.

After she had arrived in California she worked on new drawings and some sculptures and landed a one man show in a downtown gallery.

"Sidney Van Wyke," he shook her hand. "I like your work a lot," explaining that he was the art critic for the *San Francisco Daily*.

He looked at every piece in a way that made her nervous. With a hum in his throat he asked her to stay with him so he could ask questions. At last tired of his technical probes she said I don't ever like to explain, just feel. At that moment he looked at her carefully, running his eyes freely over her face and breasts and asked, "I'd like to see more. At your studio?"

He explained he was too busy in the day time. Wednesday night okay? At eight? She nodded and took a large a gulp of the cheap gallery wine.

This was before Avis moved to town and before she had found Jessica. She had to make no explanations to anyone. When she opened the door she found him dressed in a black business suit and a white shirt and tie. He was exactly her height. In the hall light he looked even more handsome. He bowed, taking her hand to kiss and she looked to see if he had clicked his heels as she suppressed a giggle. He followed her through the living room to her studio up above the street and with windows on three sides. "Romantic spot," he said. As she pulled out her drawings he took off his jacket, then his tie. He sat on the model's stool and took off his shoes . . . everything slowly, laying them neatly over the chair and the shoes neatly under, all the while commenting with enthusiasm over her work. She stopped, lay down her drawing book and watched him with astonishment, but not fear, as he took off his trousers. But in case, she moved back toward the doorway. When he was naked she had no time to scream. He had quickly embraced her. As his mouth pressed hers he lifted her in her arms laying her on the couch to undress her, all the while his insistent lips danced over hers. It was his assumption and raw desire that made her wild about him.

Many months later they both confessed love and she asked him why they could never go out, even to a distant town for supper or maybe even a weekend up to Tahoe or someplace along the ocean. And why he came only at night. He said he must never be seen, it must never get back to Eleanor, his wife. And Hazel was the only extra marital affair he had ever had.

"Would she divorce you?" She said with hope.

"Worse. She has power. She would see to it that I would never have another job as art critic and that is all I can imagine doing. What I know."

Soon he even wanted the apartment dark. He wanted her to open the door in the dark and be naked in the dark and she was to run from him and hide, like the game blind-man's bluff, he would grope to find her and take her, wherever she was hiding. She was too old to be uncomfortable so she laid pillows in the secret places.

She knew she was not supposed to go to art openings and be friendly to him. But she thought certainly it was all right to speak to him, after all he had written a splendid review of her work. One opening she dressed in a robe sort of thing from India with mirrors sewed all along the long skirt and the high waist that gave her breasts a balcony for display. She sprinkled Christmas

43

sparkles in her hair. Her lipstick had an apple flavor that kept her licking her lips with pleasure, letting her tongue slowly explore out to the corners. He tried to ignore her. *But his eyes couldn't.*

She stood near him in the midst of a group with maybe the artist or maybe his wife. He turned his back to talk to another group. "I'd like to talk with you later," he said in an official way. The next Wednesday he came late.

She was waiting impatiently with excruciating desire. They made love, not once but three times in different parts of her apartment. Before he left he turned on the kitchen lights which were so bright they seemed like police lights, consuming any equilibrium she might have had. "This is terrible for me also but it would be more so if my wife even had a hint of my deception and she kept asking about who that woman was that glowed all over as if she knew you. I told you there is no one more vindictive than she. She threw her own father out of the house when he criticized something in her paper. She's a tyrant and would destroy me and you."

He took Hazel in his arms and said, "Passion like ours had to be only temporary."

"What?"

"I can't see you anymore."

She screamed at him as he ran down the steps and out the door to the street and his car.

She sculpted for many months the lovers entangled and with precision their faces, but when her sculptures were exhibited in the Cathedral of the Redeemer, though she went every day during the month, he never appeared. He never saw her tribute to him.

Him who made love like a god but was a fallen angel . . . Demagogue, hypocrite, yet she still loved him. Maybe . . . yes, this would happen, they would meet again. Be lovers again.

A truck driver left them off near Tahoe the next morning. In a coffee and doughnut place, Avis said to her, "Don't worry, Mom my SSI goes in the bank and if we sleep out a lot we can do okay on that."

"Sure. Look we're free and we can use her pamphlets when we come to a town."

They sat in the heat drinking water. Hazel was dozing but woke when Avis asked her, "tell me again what you felt like when you found Jessica. I mean the details."

"I didn't recognize her. I saw this person, cup in hand, begging and wearing some Mumu thing and she said *hello* first."

"That's the part I didn't remember. Did she say, hello Mom?"

"No, she said, 'sinner, read this pamphlet."

"Then you knew."

"I threw my arms around her and the cup of money fell and she was flustered but she knew who I was. She didn't cry. I did but she kissed me. And for many months after that she came to visit me but every week and her entire conversation was trying to convert me."

"She's sick," Avis said. "Let's swim in the lake. No one is in sight."

The cold water was invigorating on their naked bodies and Avis yelled with delight.

Hazel thought of her sculptures, now in the hands of Jessica. She would destroy them in some way, chop them up, smash them, or just put them on the street on cleanup day . . . Hazel should have given them to a museum. She should have called one of her old students, what was his name? She would remember. It would just take time. He was a lawyer. He would help her. The next night she couldn't sleep, they found themselves only thirty miles east of the lake . . . she was worried about her children all alone, sitting in her basement condemned and waiting for her to save them from Jessica.

They walked long hours hungry and as dusk arrived they bedded down again in a field.

Hazel couldn't sleep and leaned against an oak tree beside her daughter. They got a ride to a small town where Avis tried to cash a check but nobody would.

"Avis ?"

"Yeah?"

"We might starve out here."

"I don't think so. You have to believe."

"What should we do?"

"Get to Salt Lake City as soon as possible."

"But a lot of them are Mormons. They won't want to give to Reverend Cloud."

"So we'll have to go farther east."

"I don't like the east," Hazel said.

"Now you tell me. So we should be going south."

"What's in the south?"

"Mexico, "Avis said. "Let's start hitchhiking."

"I'm afraid of Jessica."

"Mom, what are you talking about? She won't find us."

"I mean I can't desert them."

"Who?"

"My children."

"What are you telling me. You had illegitimate children?"

"Those in hell, limbo and paradise."

"We're not giving up our freedom for statues, Mom?"

Silently They walked again for two miles or so. Nobody picked them up as huge cross-country trucks raced by. "Don't worry things will be different. You will come see me from now on. I will tell her she has to let you," Hazel said. "I have to go home to take care of my . . ."

She could hardly walk anymore. She sat on the side of the road while Avis hitchhiked for them. "I want to see they were safe."

"Mom? We are free."

She wanted to see her lover. She would be daring and call him. They would be together again. He would see the sculpture she had done of them. Maybe he would leave his wife. Yes he would leave her and they would live near Golden Gate Park and watch the seals or Carmel with colorful shops. And he would be her agent and find her galleries and write up the exhibits . . .

It was nighttime when she turned the key and slipped in. But Jessica heard her and came running, screaming even before she reached the bottom step. Hazel yelled back, "I came back to take care of the children."

Jessica bounded off the last step but controlling herself into an almost silent voice that she used on her victims, "How dare you just leave? Didn't you ever consider how worried I'd be? Leave a stupid note and not consider how I would feel?"

"You did that to me for years."

"Is this revenge? I was a child. And now I sweat day and night to help others and you . . . and you just go have a lark, run off, irresponsible, thoughtless you and Avis."

"Why shouldn't we have fun? We swam in Lake Tahoe. You should go off and have fun too, honey." She tried not to be frightened.

"Fun. You tell me how?" She screwed up her face into a sarcastic grin. "With every thing I have to do. More. More. More sinners. It never stops." She was screaming again.

"Quit."

"Quit. Are you nuts?"

"Quit."

"I can't quit. I have no other life. No place to go, no other job I'd be fit for."

"Quit, Jessica."

Jessica began to flail her arms. "You made it impossible for me to have another life, a normal life, learn a job, go on to graduate school. You abandoned me."

"I abandoned *you?*"

"Letting them kidnap me and letting them keep me prisoner until I had nothing else."

"You wouldn't get off the bus."

"Why didn't you jump on the bus?"

"We were blocked."

"You didn't struggle, push fight. Fight for my life."

"They slammed the door."

"Bull shit."

She had never heard Jessica use words like that. "We hired a detective but he couldn't find you."

"Then hire another one."

"We didn't think of that."

"You ruined my life, you and Dad."

Jessica was coming toward her in a threatening way, her fist raised. She had to think fast, couldn't run. No strength left. Panic rose in her mouth. She floundered in her pocket. She found what she was searching for, drew it out, opened her palm and reached toward her daughter.

"It's okay, honey, you'll see. It will be okay."

Jessica looked at Hazel's hand and stopped, a stunned calm came over her.

"It's okay, honey, you'll see. It's okay." Hazel tiptoed toward her with a half of bar of Swiss chocolate, and Jessica slowly opened her hand to receive the sweet mesmerizing gift, the offering from her mother . . . only from her mother.

End.

WHY DO MEN DIE ON ME

*L*egs dead, bones crumbling, gut gassed, Vernon was dying. He didn't believe it. He bought a van. The brakes and shift were on the steering wheel and the seat extra cushioned for his hemorrhoids. But ten minutes down the road he realized he couldn't make it from New Jersey to Florida on his own. His cancer had become a flooding river.

Doesn't take much imagination to guess who he called. -Where are you?- I asked.

-I closed on my house but the people are letting me stay here until Tuesday. Where's Timo? I need him to drive me down.-

He really wanted *me*. Five years we've been exes, twenty-nine years we were married, married right after World War 11. And the truth is he hasn't let go the torch one itty-bit. Does he confess this? Not on your life.

He was devastated when I told him to leave, though he pretended he was glad when I knew his nether region was shriveling to an acorn at the news. On the other hand even before our divorce making the lazy ding-dong rise and shine was like shoveling through rocks to plant a rose.

Timo had taken off from work. He had saved up his vacation and was about to go ski alone. No mention of a girl friend, though once I glimpsed a pair of black panties draped over the shower in his apartment in Greenwich village. Timo says he doesn't want me to get into it. But he knows perfectly well I respect his privacy. Probably just wants to be sure the girl is special enough to introduce her to me.

But he liked to talk to me about work, stocks and bonds, and mountain climbing that sometimes we did together. Though my eyes glazed over at the financial stuff I just loved to hear his sensuous voice, like Vernon's. Yes, Timo and I have a fabulous mother son relationship, same as I have with Larry and Silvie. It's embarrassing when my friends hear how much they adore me when a lot of mothers have such bad relationships with their children.

Anyway, Timo being the youngest caved in. -Sure, Dad. I'll drive.-

Silvie and Larry knew better how to maneuver away from singing every note the old man was conducting. He tried to suppress the kids like he tried to suppress me. This is the 1980s for godsake, he couldn't suppress and get away with it. Anyway the kids are so nice they defend him, Mom, you got it all wrong . . . bla bla bla.

But the last minute Vernon changed his mind.-We're flying,- he said to Timo.

-Dad, fly? I don't think so.-

I'm sure Vernon swore up and down and yelled, you're goddamned afraid of everything, but Timo said his father said, -No sweat.-

Vernon had called Silvie. She's the middle one and very kind. But he must have known the answer, with her two kids. Anyway if she had gone, he would have had to hear her God talk . . . which he claimed was my fault as a Methodist preacher's kid. Yeah but where did he think she learned her kindness?

Vernon never went to services.

-Where did anybody get the idea that some God was going to save you? You have to save yourself.-

Actually I admired him for that, like the time when we had stopped at a red light in New York City and a creep with a gun opened our door *screaming, get out* but Vernon quietly said,—Suck it,—and sped through the red light.

Oh yeah Vernon could act brave but wasn't really. Right after I threw him out and he moved 65 miles south to the Jersey shore and discovered his cancer, coward that he was, he asked Larry to come and kill him.

Help him out was how he put it.

I grabbed Larry, -Don't go, he means for you to kill him.-

-Mom, come on. He doesn't even have a gun.-

-What do you bet? Everybody has a gun these days.-

What was Vernon thinking? Get his own son to kill him and let Larry end up in jail for murder? What twisted distorted . . . but then Vernon ups and decides to build a house and move to Florida. Silvie claims he never asked her to drive to Florida. He just said, -hay baby come on down soon as I get the ice maker running, soon as the pool is in, bring Joseph and Mary.- But I don't believe that's all he said. I know he told her she should accompany him to Florida, leave the kids with her husband, the numb-skull that he is. Not her husband, her father. But she stood her ground that's my girl. I raised them to be respectful, to have empathy that's why they didn't trash their father.

Larry couldn't help Vernon drive to Florida, he was away selling in France. His card business was taking off, cards that made me laugh out loud, like six recipes for cat stew or save a bird, lick a pussy. He inherited his humor and love of sex from me.

Vernon's house in Passe Grille was nearly finished, a little one floor job, not like our wonderful rambling Victorian house that we lived in for twenty-five years in Chatham N.J., and that he made me sell in the divorce. Our kitchen, oh man the gadgets he bought, the Cuisine Art had just come on the market, an electric fish poacher, a wall oven with a timer, a crock pot, an electric carving knife, an electric can opener, electric ice grinder, and then of all things that nobody needs, an electric tooth brush. The gadgets disgusted me since I was brought up to abhor materialism. This gourmet cooking was too much for me. I stayed thin and he got fat. But he was handsome. I could see in his eyes how he felt about the spin and hum of his gadgets the same as when he used to want to hear me spin and hum beneath him.

I couldn't wait until he left the kitchen and I could get my hands on him.

Because I also was brought up to be generous I let him take all the gadgets to his house at the Jersey shore where he kept on cooking and gaining pounds, even when he was in a wheelchair from his cancer. No doubt cooked for bimbos he surely had been collecting, though Timo, the doubter, said, -How do you know, mom?-

I would have stayed with him if he hadn't been so stubborn and had lost weight or stopped ridiculing me for going to New York and handing out blankets to the homeless, but mostly if he had only made love when I wanted. Why should I have to chase him around the house and almost beg him? Yet when he paid attention, what a lover!

Silvie says she feels sorry for him, not accepting God. Well so do I. I Think of all the love I had to give him that he wouldn't take.

So Vernon realized he had to go by plane. He put an ad in the paper for a practical nurse to accompany him. Three weeks ago this was.

The nurse was to stay with him as long as it took him to settle in his new house.

He chose Cora, a barrel of a woman with a protruding shelf behind, unruly hair, and candy green eyes, motherly enough, he thought. He hated over powering women. She seemed tuned into him and was sweet-talking, called him, Baby, even while asking for half her pay before she stepped foot on the plane.

Vernon gave her the money. Vernon, who thought all mankind was basically evil and wouldn't vote for a president unless he thought he was corrupt, -Otherwise how would he know how to steer through corruption in government?-

When they landed Cora wheeled him to the rent-a-car desk and told him she had to go pee and he sat there holding three of his tom-toms (That had been his business, manufacturing toy tom-toms) to hang on his spanking new living room wall.

He sat and waited. He sat and sat. He looked around when all of a sudden he sees Cora headed for the automatic outside doors, her suitcase in hand. He raced in his wheel chair, hollering, "Cora." Squeezing the tom-toms between his legs as he hollered, -Get out of my way,- to the milling people, and Cora hearing, ran out the door and down the side walk, bloody deserting him, leaving him with a dirty diaper in the middle of the grand concourse of the Miami airport.

So Vernon and I met after World War II when we were in Berlin with The Friends Service Committee to help rebuild the devastated city. That was the only time Vernon held a shovel. The only time I ever saw him giving his time outside his tom-tom business.

The shorts did it. Those legs. He never lost those gorgeous legs, not even now. We were magnets to each other, his legs my breasts that still pass the pencil test . . . (if your breasts swing too low they will hold a pencil up under) but mine never could, never will.

Another night we didn't make it was six years ago at Thanksgiving. Larry came home from college and right into our bedroom. Didn't knock. Vernon jumped off me like escaping a roaring fire and I sat up holding the sheet to my chin, like you see in the movies.

There was Larry in tight chinos and a cotton shirt, open to the waist, and spilling into this tangle of blond chest hairs sparkled a gold necklace. He was wearing Molly Malone high heels. He flipped a wrist at us.

-Guess what, Mom and Dad, I'm a flaming homo.-

Vernon jumped out of bed. Pulled on his underwear.

-Son, -Vernon said, -what took you so long?- Tears leaked out of his eyes as he gave Larry his famous bear hug that once broke one of my mother's ribs. Tears, bear hugs. -I love you.-

-But no grandkids,- I murmured. -You could have expressed that differently,- Vernon said. Larry laughed. -You can't stand to be called grandma anyway.-I know why Vernon went over board for Larry, to show me up. When I'm the liberal. Then Vernon had the nerve to buy Larry another gold necklace, this time to sparkle tight against his Adam's apple. Yet what parent on this earth would have encouraged that behavior?

Well it was when Larry finished college and hung out at home that Vernon's true colors showed -If you are going into business with me I suggest you take out the earring.- Vernon pretended he was just being realistic.

-But Dad, my ears will get cold.-

He always was our funniest kid. Even Vernon laughed.

He didn't join the tom-tom business. The morning Larry was leaving to live with his latest love in Hoboken we played a joke on Vernon. Vernon liked to use the downstairs bathroom. He had bought a pneumatic toilet seat from Sweden. Larry was in the bathroom. Vernon calls out -Do you mind getting off my Poop station? What in hell are you doing in there so long?-

-I don't think it is any of your business,- Larry answered in his newly developed mash potato accent.

-Get out.- Vernon was coming to the end of his rope in general. Larry complained about his fathers smoking, ran around the house opening windows, his drinking, the fatty food he cooked, the pot belly he grew . . . the same things I told him all the time.

Vernon shouted again through the bathroom door, -There are plenty of godammed others bathrooms in this house.-

Then we hear Larry laugh. -Daddy, Darling, who would ever want to get off this pneumatic seat?-

I heard this from the living room where I was reading. I got up just in time to see Larry, six-five, quietly step out. Vernon rushed in.

-Let's play a joke,- Larry said, though he claimed later that it was my idea.

I came up from the cellar with two hammers and plenty of nails and we go bang, bang, nail the door in place. Vernon inside. Vernon tried to push the door open but it was too late. Nailed in tight as a coffin. Larry and I ran out in the yard, jumping up and down, arms around each other laughing, still hearing him shout, until the door broke. That's when Larry, sped away in his Chevy, all painted in swirling colors, -Call you,- he shouted.

And I turned to Vernon coming out the back door. -Stop being so mad all the time, Vernon. It was just a joke. You know how funny Larry is.-

Vernon stormed back in the house to put on his coat for work.

But I hunted him down. Let's heat up the Wesson oil for *all the old familiar places,*—I sang.

-You must be kidding. I'm late to work because of your idiot ideas.

-But what difference does that make? It's your own business. Let's go upstairs.- I was winding my leg around him.

-Are you crazy? Can't you see how mad I am. When are you going to grow up?-

-Grow up? I'm the one with the master's degree and Phi Beta Kappa.-

-A baby with a brain. What the hell good is that?-

-Every time I put out the palm branch, you stamp on it.-

-You don't know what's appropriate,—Vernon yelled.

-It was Larry's idea. Pretty Please?-

He was getting in the car. -I know perfectly well it wasn't Larry's idea and you're a nag.-

Out the driveway. Gone.

Vernon wheeled, angry as hell, out the airport doors. Hot, sweating, his luggage on his lap, and hailed a cab. He knew without a nurse he'd have to spend one night in a motel, then file the papers for occupancy of his new house. He felt sick and weaker than ever. He kept trying to get his breath even in the air conditioned cab. The motel he chose was about six blocks from his house. The cab driver had a struggle getting him out and into his room and the motel owners asked who was staying with him and he said, I'm fine.

In the night, I mean even before the night Vernon couldn't move, get his clothes off. He lay on the bed in a sweat and finally fell asleep.

I should have known. It started on our honeymoon on the ship to England, the quiet, boring sea, the perfect place to have the best sex in the world, so we made love before breakfast, at siesta time, at night before bed. I was in heaven.

But a week later he wanted to slow down. His excuses you wouldn't believe I'm tired tonight. I have a headache.

-Are we in a soap opera?- I sobbed.

-Molly, it's like this. You buy a new car. You want to drive it as much as you can. Every time you get in it's a big new thrill, but after a week or so you don't need to drive it every minute.-

Can you imagine saying that?

All I want is a good man, a man to fulfill me. That's what every woman wants. That's the only thing a woman wants.

-Maybe if you had loved God more, things would have been different, Mom,- Sylvie said.

I felt like saying God to me was my father. I can still hear his strong voice pouring out to his admiring congregation. When I was little I wished the Congregation would leave and he would be only talking to me, see only my face lifted up to him, full of love.

Then I found Vernon and if ever there were an Olympic gold medal for sex Vernon would win. It is impossible to erase him anymore than he can me. I'll give you an example. One time we were visiting a couple of friends in their converted barn in Vermont. The friends were asleep but we stayed up lying by the fire on a bearskin Rug. He was in his tennis shorts, those luxurious Greek pillar legs. I was in my Tennis shorts and barefoot. He lifted my foot and started to message. My moans were whispers first then progressively louder.—Quiet,—he whispered.

He slipped my big toe into his mouth and slathered his tongue over and under and back and forth. His lips tickled until he grasped and sucked slowly, at first almost tentatively, shyly. I was about to explode, just from toe sucking. Can you imagine? But guess what, he stopped.

-What are you doing?- I yelled.

He plunked his hand over my mouth—For Godsake, you'll wake them.-

Our hosts were more important than me. He dropped my toe and stomped to bed in one of the converted cow stalls. I slipped in beside him naked. -How dare you?,- I asked.

-It wasn't just the noise. You're too hard a nut to crack.- Imagine a husband saying that. That's when I knew he had other women. Women no doubt who faked it. Why else would he say such a thing?

Vernon used the phone by the motel bed. He called Silvie but when he heard her voice he acted fine. Can't wait to see you, honey. And she asked his new address. She was sending him some prayer books and a liquid vitamin kit with a dropper. -Get's to your blood faster, Daddy.- Then he called Timo who was hiking in Italy. He called Larry. "I'll come," Larry said, "Next week." But none of them saw him again.

I started dating right away after I threw Vernon out. I was careful, trying to find somebody the opposite from Vernon. Somebody kind and loving like I was brought up to be, unselfish and give as much lovemaking as I wanted.

I must say I had no trouble getting men. I'm not bragging that I'm beautiful; God did that. The fact is what men saw was my capacity to love, how sexy I feel all the time, how much I love sex. How much I need a man.

-God is watching, sex without marriage is a sin.
-Sylvie warned.

-Larry said,- my advice comes from my lesbian friends, women are the best-

And Timo said, -sometimes I don't feel I belong in this family. Aren't you too old for sex?-

I was hiking as much as I could. I was with the Sierra club up in Bear mountain state park and ahead of me is this compact, wooly dark haired really cute guy with a dedicated doctor's smile, eleven years younger. But guess what? He says makes no difference.

He even begged me not to dye my hair or put on makeup. I thought, wow, here's an up front guy. He didn't even try and hide the braces on his legs to keep his knees from going weird when climbing the rocks. He wasn't proud or uptight. Yeah, wait till you hear. James was a recovering alcoholic, watched everything he put in his mouth to be sure it wasn't addictive, that eventually included me.

He lived in Connecticut and I in Jersey in a dinky house I could afford after our divorce. Back and forth up and down, but mostly it's me because he's a doctor, right?.

"I'm the one with the schedule," he says.

I have to give in. But when he says he's coming to me he often cancels, emergencies. So he begs me to come live with him. He's got everything, money, humor, a gorgeous house in the woods. But I was trying not to go too fast. But I wanted to go too fast.

The next morning Vernon doesn't get up. He has soiled himself, is dehydrated. The maid knocks. He doesn't answer and finally calls the manager and they find him like that and he says, just get me a cab. But the owner calls the ambulance. Vernon doesn't like that. I'm sure he screams at them, *no*, but they take him anyway.

At the hospital he tried to throw himself off the gurney. They strapped him down. It hurts just to think about him like that, that lion, bear of man, his body decaying.

Sylvie's kids got chicken pox so she couldn't come but she calls me to go. Please Mom, he needs you. We couldn't find exactly where Timo was.

And Larry said, -I'll be dead before him.-

-What are you talking about?-

-I've got AIDS, Mom.-

I screamed, "Don't even joke about that."

I dragged the suitcases from James' cellar two years ago this was. Should I go, should I stay with James? I mean after six or seven months of his passion running on low I told him to excercise more, his biceps were sagging. He should alter his diet, more bran. More shriveling.. You buy a firmer bed. Why couldn't he wear brighter clothes. More shriveling. "*You drive the new car less, the newness wears off.*" Only James was different. He had a real problem like when I said, go left, go right, slower, harder . . . the more I talked the more *he* couldn't. He had the nerve to say, -You talk too much. If you could just be quiet and let your mouth take charge of something else.-

A twin to Vernon, thinking only of himself and not my pleasure. I told him I needed him in the morning and evening. First shrivel all the way and then he more or less hid his ding-dong, telling me it was my fault that I had pressured him, that I was the problem. Can you imagine finding another Vernon.

As I packed to go, I told him, -Have you thought of this? Since you refused what I wanted I could call you a rapist.-

He said,-What?-

My father was only fifty when he died. Now I'm older than him, though everybody says I look barely forty and if they find out I'm a grandma, god bless them, they shriek in disbelief.

My father looked young too. His beautiful curls never turned white.

Guess what, I have this hair dresser, Kelly, who keeps me this cross between red and brown. He mixes his own formula. I go late in the day. He closes up the shop. The chair goes all the way back, and believe me, he isn't gay.

Silvie says my trouble is I never had brothers. Like I didn't see enough Nether regions? She would be very surprised to know how many I've had intimate knowledge of.

Our manse had a wide front porch we loved to sit on, my sisters and I. Andrea is older and Latisha is younger. I am the middle. On Saturday afternoons, on the porch in summer my teen-age friends would come and Daddy would talk about how to make the world better. It was that era, pot and love and giving to mankind and half raw vegetables. Daddy's deep voice, rolled in our ears, luring us with words like sacrifice, blood of the lamb, fearless giving.

The girls stared into his eyes so did the boys, I was jealous of the way he included all my friends with his staring back at each and every one. Seeing them as individuals.

Afterwards I teased, -So are we all equal?-

-Come on Molly, don't be that way.-

Then I felt guilty I loved my sisters and girlfriends. But I just, well, loved him the most.

He was so beautiful with his pale face, his strong thin body and his pretense of vigor.

-You look beat.- I said. -Daddy let me massage your tired muscles.- At first he protested. He just wanted to have a nap but I kept after him. -I'll make you feel better. Please.- and he laid down on the couch in his study. I shut the door from the noise of my mother vacuuming. He lay on his stomach and I asked him to take his shirt off. I'll be right back. I ran to get my skin lotion and when I poured some into my hands I could see that he was almost asleep. I messaged his neck and shoulders. He groaned with pleasure. I was so happy. I worked my fingers, still lightly across and down his shoulder blades and warm knobs of his spine. I ran my hands down his smooth arms and into his hands. His hands thrilled me. I remembered his hands as he dressed me for kindergarten. My mother's hands were rougher. I turned to the small of his back. I put my hands under his belt. He jumped up. -What are you doing?- I was ashamed. But why? I just wanted to feel the warmth of his skin. Not allowing myself any special words for the feeling.

After that he treated me like an outcast, never drove me any where unless my sisters or friends came along. He left me, my father deserted me.

A few days before I married Vernon, Daddy and I were out in the yard alone talking about flowers to cut for the house and I asked him, -Why were you so cool and distant to me all these years?-

He paused to think of the words. -I guess, Molly, because you wouldn't stop . . . I mean you came out of the shower with no clothes on and ran to your room, pretending you didn't want me to see you, wore deep cut blouses. Wore skirts too short with your legs open. I tried to get your mother to say something but you know how shy she is.

I threw my arms around him weeping and then I kissed him on the mouth and he let me . . . oh God he let me. I was in heaven.

I won't go into how I met Eliah about three years ago. Kid psychologist. I'd never even known a psychologist, never gone to one in my life. Actually I thought of them as charlatans and that was accurate for Eliah.

Eliah opened the door in his stocking feet. Turns out he saw his clients in stocking feet. He was very tall with short grey hair at forty-three and deep set brown eyes. I felt scared and awkward -I'm not here for a session,- I explained. -I am friends with your niece.-

-My niece has gone back to Isreal.

"Really?"

"Sorry, but come in. I'm having my lunch break.-

Sitting at a round glass table in the glitzy apartment where in a slit between buildings you could see the East river, he said -So why are you really here?-

-Pardon me.-

-Okay, I'll put it another way. What's troubling you?

-Do I look like a person with troubles?-

-You're beautiful so that's already one strike against you.-
The way he said it made me ashamed.

He leaned back in his chair and waited while almost hypnotizing me with his eyes. Why was I putting up with this? Why did I stay? It had been a long time, maybe never, somebody was that quiet, absolutely with not a muscle moving, paying attention to me. His eyes made me feel unstable, and yet grateful. He folded his hands and waited.

He waited for me to stop crying. I doubled my head into my lap. I was in agony. He got up and handed me the box of kleenex. Then he drew me from the glitzy chair to the couch and sat beside me on the couch. He quietly took my hand. -Don't hurry. I'm here for you.-

I couldn't even think of a beginning so my words cascaded, -All I want is to find a man to make love as often as I want. Think about me for once. There must be such a man It's simple. I'm simple. I would be fulfilled and happy.- He stayed in a frozen animal way as if listening to signs of danger and then he drew my face to his and kissed me.

Can you imagine that fast? But there is something real and true about love at first sight. I didn't think the bliss would ever go away. We made love, every week, sometimes twice a week and I'd bring in a whole whole roasted chicken and we'd eat in bed afterwards and listen to his taped weekly psychological broadcasts on the radio and people called in needing answers to their problems. Like my father had had people into his study, I told him.

Then we would lay the leftovers on his side table and he would begin asking me what I wanted, in detail.

-To the left, softer, harder, stay on my breasts. Kiss me. No again, bite my lip, tickle my ears.-

He said with pride -You've found a man who will make love to you the way you want and as long as you want.-

But my eyes were open about Eliah. The radio stuff. Phone calls came in from his producer and director and bla bla,bla, on and on and even when he turned on the answering phone I hated the sound of the ring and the voice on the speaker invading. And one day I stopped in the middle and he asked what the matter was?-

It was not only the phone but I told him my list.

-I don't like that you grew a beard, your pot belly. Sometimes you snore and the apartment is too hot, if you open windows I hear the street noise.-

The next week I said what do you mean you have an appointment after lunch, break it and he said, you don't mean it. Okay, he said and we jumped back in bed and he asked, this way, that way. I'm tired of being asked, I said. But you want it right, he said. Then the phone rang, He didn't answer it, but still, it rang so I pulled it from its jack. He made love. I mean I stayed still, not my usual making love *with* him. Suddenly he jumped up and said, -this isn't about sex is it?-

-You just aren't doing it right.-

-Bull shit,- he said.

-Do you think I'm pretty? Do you like my eyes. Aren't they too small. You never tell me I'm beautiful anymore.-

-There is nothing about you I don't love.-

-Yes there is and that's why you don't give me what I want?- He laughed. He had the nerve to laugh. That's how much he respected me.

-Well I have plenty of men after me. I just have to wave a hand or give a wink. I don't need you.- I began to dress.

He thought he knew every thing about me. What an ego he had, after eighteen months. It takes a lifetime to know people. That's what psychologists don't get. Snap judgments.

-This isn't about sex,- he said again and then he got out of bed and standing there like he was a God, all naked, with his little winnie old and wrinkled and said to me, -It's sad. I hope you'll listen and we can get through your self destructive. I made love to you because I love you. I made love the way you wanted. You didn't want love because you don't believe in it and that's because you don't believe in yourself. Who did this to you? Was it your father who wouldn't make love to you or your mother who always said, dear, couldn't you find a better way to comb your hair or fix your make up or get an A instead of a B or find better friends.

-Like a child you try and be obnoxious so I will spank you, or fulfill your own prophecy. How can you be satisfied, my darling, if you're not satisfied with yourself. I can help you stop that, show you how marvelous you are.-

-First you told me I was the best. You loved my love-making, my apartment, my radio programs and then when you found out I truly loved you you thought I'm not what he thinks so he'll leave me.-

-I wish your audiences could see you now, naked and raving. Come here, kiss me. Oh you're so angry.-

-Wrong. I want to help you, help us.-

-If you want to help us. Make love right now.-

-I can't make love until I calm down. This isn't the right moment.-

-You mean you don't want me.-

-You're becoming impossible. Why can't you trust me?-

-So all you've cared about was analyzing me?-

-That's what I mean about trust.-

-So it's all my fault. You're sick, and I was going to tell you that I heard last week that Larry is HIV positive. I was going to get you to console me, but you're too self-centered for that, too big, important charlatan all mighty god. Goodbye.-

-Please,- he begged. -don't throw us away. I want to talk to you about Larry.

-Too late.-

-How did it get too late?. What happened? I'll do anything.-

So now the know it all aint so know it all. No you're too sick. I'll show you how sick you are.-

I picked up the phone and threw it out the window with a bunch of papers on his desk and an ink well and he screamed at me,

-Get out. You are too destructive for me.-

This is the kind of guy he was, in the end, panty-waist hot shot. Wanted his papers more than me, his phone and his papers, more than me!

I didn't see him again. You would have thought he might have called me and apologized. A man who is influencing children and parents. My God. I'm glad I got out. This may sound weird but it is from my forgiving up bringing. I still love him. I still want him. If only he'd been unselfish and more loving to me.

I got this phone call from Mom. She was as usual, calm as a cucumber, those slow words sticking to the roof of her mouth.

-Molly, your father is in the hospital.-

Dad was a half day away, up in this rinky-dink hospital near Albany. Daddy was dying, two years after we were married. I left little Larry with Vernon. By then Vernon was running his business so he didn't mind baby-sitting. But he let crawling Larry do anything he damned pleased, like later I found out that Larry had been splashing his hands in the toilet while Vernon was sitting in a chair reading the paper.

Daddy was hooked up to tubes, clear plastic coming out of his nose, intravenous attached to his arm. Mom holding his other hand and patting it. Out, he was out, gone. I kissed his closed eyes. But I didn't cry. It was too terrible even to cry.

But when Mom went out of the room for a little break I gently pulled his lids open just so I could see his chestnut brown eyes one last time. a dead stare at me, a concentrated stare, dead but mine. Those eyes were mine, never moving away. Maybe he would see me, somewhere from the world of spirit and love.

I jumped, Mom had a hold of my shoulder. She could creep up unbeknownst. When we were kids, we liked to pee under the forsythia bush, like a magic ritual, and she'd sneak up on us and wag a witch like finger. Freaked us out.

I turned around. She was doing that right at me. -You know why your father is in this state?-

-No,- I gasped out.

-He took energy pills and they gave him a stroke. You know why he took energy pills?-

-I guess because he wanted energy.- I knew that didn't sound good.

-Because of you.-

I shivered. -I don't get it.-

-You were the hiker of the family. He always said when he retired he wanted to climb with you.-

-He wanted to climb with me?-

-There probably could have been a way for you to show him he was okay as a father.- What did she mean? What did she know?

-I know you won't answer that,- she said. -But something happened between you.-

Daddy died. He's here with me like a closed box and the key is gone. And I keep thinking I'll find the key. I keep thinking he will come and save me. He represented our Savior, after all. He was in direct line for saving. That was some years before our divorce and my seeking the perfect man.

Why do men die on me?

Finally Eliah wrote a letter, I'll give him that. He didn't call and he wrote just one sentence. "I love you and I want you when you feel good enough about yourself to let me." -Can you imagine, as if everything was my fault. A perfect bastard and I don't even want to say a typical man.

I tried for two days to find Vernon in Florida. He had been moved to a different hospital. He was in a bad way. I could hardly recognize him. The big, rough, ruddy face was rock grey, his lips milk colored, his hair wispy. His brow, no longer scowling, the wrinkles ironed I inched near the equipment around him that seemed to be waiting to resgester his death, heart monitors, oxygen. There was a someone sitting in a chair beside him.

She stood, a tiny forceful woman and said in a smooth voice, -I'm from hospice.-

-From hospice?- I leaned over Vernon. -What for? You don't need that.-

He was so frail that even when I sat on the edge of the bed he winched. -You don't need that, you have to live.- I blinked my eyes to stem the tears. I saw Vernon in his prime with that booming voice, his anger and passion rising red across the bridge of his nose and turning his eyes black.

-What did you do to yourself. I told you you weren't eating right, all that fried goop and what about the amount of sweets and the lack of-

-This is no time. I need it quiet and peaceful-

-Look at what happened to you Vernon. We have to work on you living. We have to get you out of here. We could start over. I'd be willing to stay in Florida.-

-I think you better leave now. There is nothing more to say, Molly. It's over.-

The hospice nurse, moved in closer, her shoulders with a scary bull stance. But she wasn't going to scare me.

He whispered, -wait tell me about the children. I didn't want to tell him about Larry and HIV . . . which of course was Vernon's fault for applauding that he was gay. But you have to think of being kind so I told him about his illness.

-I just want to die first,- Vernon said.

-Vernon you got to live. We have so much love-making to catch up on.-

-Did you come here to get in the last ditch nagging?- He tried so hard to boom at me but a trickle of sound came.

-No, no, I came to see you and I thought you'd be glad and to tell you I'm sorry that I threw you out.-

-What are you talking about? I left you.-

-Of all times to lie to me.-

-Would you please get off my bed. Can't a man die in peace? Nurse, please.-

She rushed at me. -This way.-

She tried to take my arm. I swung around and my elbow hit her breast.

-Out, now.-

-I'm his wife.-

-Ex.- Vernon tried a pathetic shout.

-He's out of his head. He wants me to stay. He couldn't bear for me to leave him. He just wants to spare me seeing him like this, always thinking of me.-

-Take her away.- He said this with such passion I got dizzy, light-headed, extremely sparked up. I ran back and threw myself on his chest. I knew what he was doing giving me a spark, his passionate feeling about me.

-No,- I shouted this time. The nurse wasn't there. But I soon found out why. In she came with another nurse, bluntly a dike with worked on muscles. They grabbed me on either side and an alarm went off down the hall. And some huge type guard ran at me, took my arm, his hand like a robot clamp and dragged me toward the elevator. I couldn't say anything to Vernon. I called even after the guard closed us in the elevator. I screamed in his ear, -Have you ever had a loved one die, have you?-

-Sorry, ma'm, the air will make you feel better.-

The air? on this hot street as I'm pacing, looking for something, maybe a cab, a place to live. Maybe a place to lie down and close my eyes. Fury is clenching my heart, soldering my breath into gasps.

How dare they shove me away from my beloved husband? What kind of people are they? I should have called the hospital director, called the police, 911, someone, anyone.

Look how inured with cruelty the world has become. I'm glad my father isn't alive to see. Nobody preserves love. There was love in the old days. Now its destroy, tear down, bomb into ashes. I'm so tired. I'm going to lie down here on the curb. Then someone will find me and take me back to the hospital so that I can be with the only person who made perfect love.

End

J. Carol Goodman lives with her husband Ted in Williamstown Ma. where she writes, paints, gardens and makes Thanksgiving dinner for kids and grandkids.